"**Jill Murphy deserves a constellation of gold stars for consistently writing picture books that please children and enrapture parents.**" *Observer*

When Jill Murphy penned the first of the Large Family series over 30 years ago, little did she know that her elephants would speak to so many, the stories going on to sell over five million copies worldwide. Today, numerous awards and a television adaptation later, they ring as true as ever, and continue to be celebrated for their beautifully observed depiction of hectic, warm – but ultimately ordinary – family life.

THIS BOOK BELONGS TO:

....

First published 1993 by Walker Books Ltd
87 Vauxhall Walk, London SE11 5HJ

This edition published 2017

2 4 6 8 10 9 7 5 3 1

© 1993 Jill Murphy

The right of Jill Murphy to be identified as
author/illustrator of this work has been asserted by her
in accordance with the Copyright, Designs and Patents Act 1988

This book has been typeset in Bembo Educational

Printed in China

British Library Cataloguing in Publication Data:
a catalogue record for this book is available from the British Library

ISBN 978-1-4063-7072-0

www.walker.co.uk

A Quiet Night In

Jill Murphy

WALKER BOOKS
AND SUBSIDIARIES
LONDON • BOSTON • SYDNEY • AUCKLAND

"I want you all in bed early tonight,"
said Mrs Large. "It's Daddy's birthday
and we're going to have a quiet night in."
"Can we be there too?" asked Laura.
"No," said Mrs Large. "It wouldn't be
quiet with you lot all charging about
like a herd of elephants."
"But we *are* a herd of elephants," said Lester.
"Smartypants," said Mrs Large. "Come on
now, coats on. It's time for school."

That evening, Mrs Large had
the children bathed and in their
pyjamas before they had even had
their tea. They were all very cross.
"It's only half past four," said Lester.
"It's not even dark yet."
"It soon will be," said Mrs Large grimly.

After tea, the children set about making
place cards and decorations for the
dinner table. Then they all tidied up.
Then Mrs Large tidied up again.

Mr Large arrived home looking very tired.

"We're all going to bed," said Lester.

"So you can be quiet," said Laura.

"Without us," said Luke.

"Shhhh," said the baby.

"Happy Birthday," said Mrs Large. "Come and see the table."

Mr Large sank heavily into the sofa. "It's lovely, dear," he said, "but do you think we could have our dinner on trays in front of the TV? I'm feeling a bit tired."

"Of course," said Mrs Large. "It's *your* birthday.
   You can have whatever you want."
"We'll help," said Luke.
   The children ran to the kitchen and brought two trays.
"I'll set them," said Mrs Large. "We don't want
   everything ending up on the floor."

"Can we have a story before we
    go to bed?" asked Luke.

"Please," said Lester.

"Go on, Dad," said Laura. "Just one."

"Story!" said the baby.

"Oh, all right," said Mr Large.

"Just one, then."

   Lester chose a book and they all
cuddled up on the sofa.

Mr Large opened the book and began to read:
"One day Binky Bus drove out of the big garage.
'Hello!' he called to his friend, Micky Milkfloat – "
"I don't like that one," said Laura. "It's a boy's story."
"Look," said Mr Large, "if you're going to argue about it,
you can all go straight to bed without *any* story."
So they sat and listened while Mr Large read to them.

After a while he stopped.

"Go on, Daddy," said Luke.

"What happened after he
bumped into Danny Dustcart?"

"Did they have a fight?" asked Lester.

"Look," said Laura. "Daddy's asleep."

"Shhhh!" said the baby.

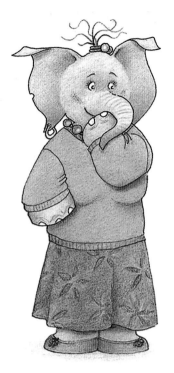

Mrs Large laughed. "Poor Daddy," she said.
"Never mind, we'll let him snooze a bit longer
   while I take you all up to bed."
"Will you just finish the story, Mum?" asked Lester.
"We don't know what happens in the end," said Luke.
"Please," said Laura.
"Story!" said the baby.

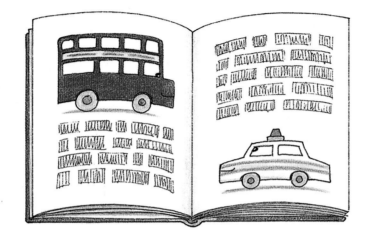

"Move up, then," said Mrs Large. She picked up the book and began to read: "'Watch where you're going, you silly Dustcart!' said Binky. Just then, Pip the Police Car came driving by…"

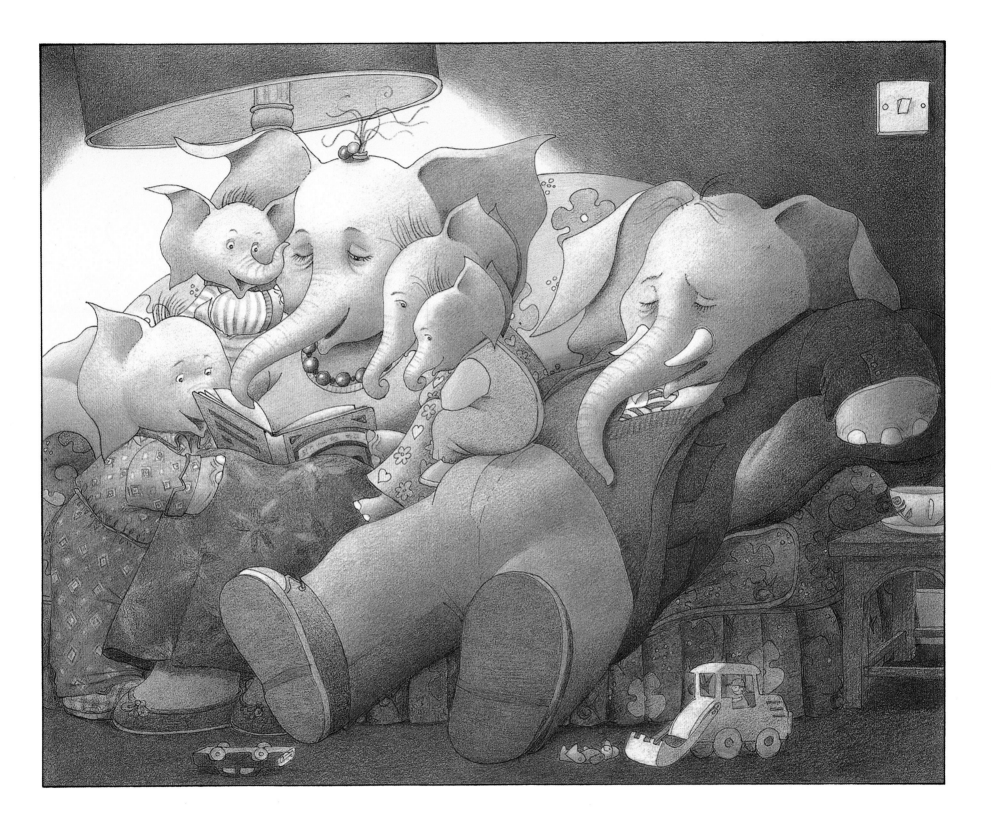

After a while, Mrs Large stopped reading.

"What's that strange noise?" asked Lester.

"It's Mummy snoring," said Luke. "Daddy's snoring too."

"They must be very tired," said Laura, kindly.

"Shhhh!" said the baby.

The children crept from the sofa and fetched a blanket.

They covered Mr and Mrs Large and tucked them in.

"We'd better put ourselves to bed,"
  said Lester. "Come on."
"Shall we take the food up with us?"
  asked Luke. "It *is* on trays."
"It's a pity to waste it," said Laura.
"I'm sure they wouldn't mind. Anyway,
  they wanted a quiet night in."
"Shhhh!" said the baby.

JILL MURPHY

is one of Britain's most treasured author-illustrators, who created her first book, the bestselling *The Worst Witch*, while still only eighteen. She is best known for her award-winning Large Family series – a series which includes *Five Minutes' Peace* and the Kate Greenaway commended *All in One Piece*.

Among Jill's very popular characters are a small monster called Marlon, who appears in the acclaimed picture books *The Last Noo-Noo* and *All For One,* and Ruby the bunny, who stars in *Meltdown!* Jill lives in Cornwall.